Chapter 1

FOR AS LONG as he could remember,
Ken's Great Grandma had lived at 37
Cedar Street. It was an old house, almost
as old as Great Grandma, with two rooms
upstairs, two rooms downstairs and a
little garden at the back. It had no
bathroom.

Everybody wanted to do something
about Great Grandma and her house,
mainly because of the bathroom. Ken's

mum thought that Great Grandma ought to go and live in a nice old folk's bungalow, and his gran thought that she should go and live with *her* because, after all, Great Grandma was *her* mum. Ken's dad was a plumber and wanted to build her a bathroom, but Great Grandma took no notice of any of them.

'I've managed here for eighty years without a bathroom,' Great Grandma said. 'Or a fridge.' Mum thought she

A SUPERCHAMP BOOK

22115722M

NDON

22115722M

For Ken

William Heinemann Ltd
Michelin House, 81 Fulham Road
London SW3 6RB

LONDON   MELBOURNE   AUCKLAND

First published 1993
Text © 1993 Jan Mark
Illustrations © Lis Toft 1993
ISBN 0 434 97665 2
Produced by Mandarin Offset
Printed in Hong Kong
The right of Jan Mark to be
identified as author of this
work has been asserted by
her in accordance with the
Copyright, Designs & Patents
Act 1988

A school pack of SUPERCHAMPS 19–24
is available from
Heinemann Educational Books
ISBN 0 435 00093 4

ought to have one of those, too, instead of the meat safe, a little wire cage that hung on the shady wall outside the kitchen door. Great Grandma still did her washing in an old copper gas boiler that lit with a terrible *whumffff* when she put a match to it.

'At least let Dave put in a washing machine,' Mum begged her. Dave was Ken's dad, and he could have done it easily, but Great Grandma took no notice of that, either, and when she grew too stiff to bend down and light the copper with a match, she made long spills out of rolled-up pages from the *Courier*. It was the local newspaper and the only one she ever read. This worried Mum and Gran even more. They were both sure that Great Grandma was all set to burn the house down.

Ken never minded about the outside loo, or the exploding copper, any more

than Great Grandma did. He liked to drop
in sometimes on his way home from
school. Great Grandma was always
pleased to see him. She would make tea
and they would sit in the kitchen and
listen to music on her little radio that
stood on the dresser. Mum and Dad had
given Great Grandma that radio on her

seventieth birthday. It was probably the newest thing in the house.

Sometimes Ken said, 'Can we look at the photos?' and Great Grandma let him go to the sideboard in the front room and fetch out the shoe box where she kept hundreds of photographs.

Gran put her snapshots in an album.

Mum and Dad had slides and Ken's Uncle Tom didn't take any photographs at all. He had a camcorder and made home videos. Great Grandma could not be bothered with any of that. For years and years, almost ninety years, she had been putting her photographs in the shoe box, any old how, so that sometimes the newest ones were at the bottom and the oldest on top. You could only tell how old they were by the clothes that people were wearing, for very few of them had dates on the back.

'Have you always had the same shoe box?' Ken asked.

'This is the third,' Great Grandma said. It still had the price on the lid: 27/11¾d.

When Ken asked Gran how old she was she told him, 'As old as my tongue and a little bit older than my teeth,' but it didn't matter. He knew how old Gran was

because in Great Grandma's shoe box was
a faded brown picture of a tiny baby in the
arms of a pretty young woman in a straw
hat. This one did have a date on the back.
Somebody had written, *Mary with
Dorothy. July 1925*. Dorothy was Gran,
and the pretty girl was Great Grandma,
proud and smiling, holding up her first
baby to be photographed.

In the holidays Ken always went round

to 37 Cedar Street on Monday mornings,
because Great Grandma still did her
washing on Mondays, just as she had
always done, and he liked to watch her
lighting the copper. Then he had to keep
an eye on it for the moment when foam

began to bubble out from under the lid
and the washing was cooked. They never
had time to look at photographs on
Mondays.

Then everything changed. One

Monday morning Ken went round to 37 Cedar Street and knocked on the door, but no one answered. He knocked again, peering through the letter box, but he couldn't see anything because Great Grandma had a curtain hanging behind the door to keep out draughts. Still no one answered although he called through the letter box. The heavy curtain caught his words and folded them up.

The white cat from next door came and sat on the step with him. This gave Ken an idea. He went and knocked at the house

next door, but nobody was answering there, either, and there was no house on the other side. Great Grandma lived on the corner, and the pavement ran along beside her garden wall, but the wall was too high for Ken to climb and it had no gate. Even though he jumped he could not get a hand-hold on top of the wall to haul himself up. In the end, after one last call through the letter box, he ran all the way to Gran's house, which was closer than his own. Grandpa was in the front garden, cutting the grass, but as soon as he saw Ken at the gate he could tell that something was wrong. He switched off the mower and hurried over.

'What's up?' he said. 'Somebody chasing you?'

'Something's happened to Great Grandma,' Ken said, gasping because he was out of breath. 'She won't answer the door.'

'Calm down,' Grandpa said, although at once he began to look worried. 'Perhaps she's gone out.'

'She never goes out on Monday

mornings,' Ken said. 'She does the washing. That's why I go round – to watch the copper.'

When Ken mentioned the copper Grandpa looked even more alarmed. 'Good thing your Granny's out,' he muttered. 'Come on, Ken, let's get round there and see what's happened.'

He sounded calm, but Ken knew how

worried he must be because he strode straight out to his car, parked by the kerb, and did not even bother to put the mower away.

It only took a few minutes to drive to Great Grandma's house. Grandpa parked round the corner, where the road was wider, and switched off the engine.

'How will you get in?' Ken asked.

'I have a spare key,' Grandpa said. 'We all do. Now, you stay here,' he told Ken. 'I don't think I'll be long, but if I am, just wait. OK?' He hurried away. Ken stayed where he was, in the back seat, trying to imagine what had happened to Great Grandma. Suppose she had finally had an accident with the copper, or fallen on the stairs? She always went up and down very slowly, but that was because she was old, not because she was careful. Now he understood why Mum and Dad and Gran had worried and fussed so much. They must feel as he felt now – all the time.

Suddenly Grandpa was back, opening the car door.

'Great Grandma's been taken ill,' he said. 'I want you to run down to the phone box and call an ambulance.'

Ken scrambled out onto the pavement.

'I haven't got any money.'

'You don't need money for an emergency. It's 999,' Grandpa said. 'Now run along. I mean it. *Run!*'

An emergency. 999 had always meant

car crashes to Ken; robberies, houses catching fire, not things that could actually happen to *him*.

He did not have far to run. There was a row of phone boxes outside the pub at the end of the street. He was afraid that the

operator would think he was mucking about because he was a child, but she put him through right away when he asked for the ambulance service, and the man who answered was kind, making sure that he had given the right address. He wanted to ring Mum, too, because he was sure she ought to know, but he wasn't certain how to do it without money. If only Great Grandma was on the telephone – but that was another thing she refused to have. 'I've lasted ninety years without one,' she always said.

Ken ran all the way back to Cedar Street where Grandpa was at the door. In the distance they could hear a siren. Perhaps that was the ambulance, already.

'Well done,' Grandpa said. 'Now, you go home and tell your mum what's happened. I think Great Grandma may have had a stroke – can you remember that?'

'Can't I help here?' Ken said.

'No, you go home. That'll be the best help. Your mum will see to things and tell your gran.'

The ambulance was coming down the
street.

'Off you go,' Grandpa said, firmly, and

Ken went, very slowly, leaving Grandpa on the doorstep with the white cat from next door, still sitting there, washing itself. He had wanted to say good-bye to Great Grandma before the ambulance took her to hospital. He was afraid he might never see her again.

Chapter 2

GREAT GRANDMA GOT better, and came out of hospital, but she did not go back to Cedar Street.

Instead she went to live with Gran and Grandpa. They turned their dining room into a bed sitting room for her, and that was all that she seemed to do now, go to bed, or sit. When she walked she needed a stick to lean on, and she did not even want to talk much any more. Worst of all, she kept forgetting who Ken was.

He found this out after the Whitsun fête. Last year they had all gone there together, but this time he went with Grandpa, Mum and Dad. Gran stayed at home with Great Grandma, because she could not be left alone.

There were sports events at the fête,

and Ken went in for the obstacle race. He had to crawl through a pipe, jump hurdles, dodge traffic cones and wriggle under a net. He was not very good at all that, but he had done a lot of fast running lately, and although he was the last one out from under the net he overtook everybody else and reached the finishing tape first of all.

Afterwards he did some more running, ahead of the rest of the family, back to Gran's house to tell her the news.

Gran and Great Grandma were in the back garden. Gran was weeding and Great Grandma was sitting on a chair, watching her.

Ken ran up the path. 'Gran! Gran! I won the race! I came first in the obstacle race.'

'Lobster race?'

'Obstacle race,' Ken said.

'What did he say?' Great Grandma
asked. She did not hear too well, these
days.

'Ken's won a race,' Gran said.

'That's nice,' said Great Grandma. 'Now you'll have your picture in the paper with all the kings and queens.'

'Well, the man from the *Courier* took our photo,' Ken said, 'but there weren't any kings and queens.'

'Oh yes,' Great Grandma said. 'A whole row of them. I remember.'

Gran frowned. 'Was there a fancy dress competiton, Ken?'

Great Grandma snorted. 'Fancy dress, my foot! It was all the kings and queens of Europe. Don't you remember, Ken, the day you won the race?'

'I only won it just now,' Ken protested. 'A couple of hours ago.'

'You'll see,' Great Grandma said, 'when the picture's in the paper.'

The *Courier* was published on Tuesdays. Ken bought a copy on the way home from school and opened it there in the street outside the newsagent's. The photographs of the fête were in the middle pages, and Ken was there with all the other people who had won races, but only the top of his head was showing and, of course, there were no kings and queens. He took the paper round to Gran's.

'Shall I show Great Grandma?' he said.

'I already showed her ours,' Gran said, 'and she's a bit upset. She says it's the wrong photo.'

'No kings and queens, you mean?' Ken said.

Great Grandma, in her bed sitting room, heard them and called out.

'Is that you, Kenny? Did you have a good day in the shop?'

'What shop?' Ken said.

'We'll be with you in a moment,

Mum,' Gran called back. Then she said, quietly, to Ken, 'You know, I've been thinking. I believe she's getting you mixed up with her brother Ken. He'd have been your Great Great Uncle.'

'I never heard of him,' Ken said. 'She never told me about her brother.' He thought about the shoe box. 'He's not in any of the photographs.'

'He died in 1917. He was a soldier in the First World War,' Gran said. 'I think she was very fond of him and it made her sad to talk about him.'

'And she thinks I'm him?' Ken said. 'Why?'

'You've got the same name, haven't you?' Gran said. 'When people get very old, they sometimes remember things that happened years ago better than things that happened last year – or even last week. When you came in on Sunday and said you'd won that race, it must have jolted Great Grandma's memory. She's been talking about Kenny, her brother, ever since. Asking me when he'll be coming home.'

'And here he is.' They both jumped and looked round. Great Grandma was standing in the doorway, leaning on her stick.

'Hello, Kenny,' she said. 'You're late.

Did they keep you at the shop?'

Ken didn't know what to say. He couldn't even say, 'Hello, Great Grandma,' because, he suddenly realised, she did not think that she was a great grandma, any more. Then he did know, and he said, 'Hello, Mary. Sorry I'm late.'

Great Grandma smiled.

'Is that the paper you've got there? Has it got your picture in it, with all the kings and queens?'

'There aren't any kings and queens,' Ken said.

'You must have got the wrong paper, then,' Great Grandma said. 'Pa *will* be disappointed. He said he had a special place for that picture. All the kings and queens of Europe, he said, and our Kenny along with them.'

'I'll look out for it,' Ken promised, but Great Grandma had turned sadly away, back into her own room. He watched her go. 'Pa will be disappointed,' she had said. That was her dad she was talking about. Ken's great great grandfather, someone he had never seen.

The house seemed suddenly to be full of ghosts.

Chapter 3

KEN WENT ON dropping in to see Gran and Great Grandma on his way home from school. Sometimes Great Grandma knew who he was, and asked about Mum and Dad and school, but more often she thought that he was her brother Kenny, who had died so long ago, just home from his work in the shop. Then she would say, 'Have you got the paper yet? Have you got the photograph with all the kings and queens?'

Ken began to wish he had never won the race, except that when they heard about it at school, and learned how he had *just* won it, at the very last moment, the PE teacher began making him practise sprints. He had never thought of himself as a runner before, and he had entered the obstacle race only for fun, but it was nice, for once, doing something where he nearly always came first. He began to think about the county championships when he was older.

Meanwhile, things were happening at Cedar Street. At last, Dad was putting in a bathroom.

'No one will take it without a bathroom, these days,' Dad said.

Ken was horrified. 'You're not going to sell Great Grandma's house, are you?'

'Of course we aren't,' Dad said. 'Anyway, it's not ours to sell. Your great grandma's lived in that house for almost all her life. But we can't leave it empty. It isn't good for houses to stand empty. They need to be lived in. We're going to decorate it.'

'And put in a bathroom?'

'That's right, upstairs at the back. Then we shall rent it to someone and your Gran will have the money to help look after Great Grandma. It will just suit a young couple without any children, though Great Grandma raised six kids there. People expect more, these days. When she dies, the house will belong to Gran anyway.'

Ken hated to think of Great Grandma dying, but he knew now that she probably would, before long. He just wished he could solve the mystery of the kings and queens for her, because he could see that she was unhappy about it.

He asked Mum and Dad if they had any ideas.

'Do you think it could be playing cards?' Mum said.

'She didn't mention jacks and jokers as well, did she?' Dad said.

'It was a photograph, in the paper,' Ken said. 'She's quite sure about that.'

'Do you know anything about this Kenny?' Dad asked Mum.

'Only that he was killed in action,' Mum said. 'He must have been quite young. I think his dad was so upset when he was killed that he got rid of anything that belonged to Kenny, so that he wouldn't be reminded all the time.'

Ken thought that this was a terrible thing to do, but no wonder there had never been any pictures of Kenny in the shoe box. If there ever had been a picture of him with all the kings and queens of Europe, that must have gone too, but what would a London lad, who worked in a shop, be doing in a photograph with kings and queens?

Dad had his own work to do during the week, but on Sundays he went along to Cedar Street. Sometimes Ken went with him to help. The little bedroom at the back of the house was empty now, the one where Great Grandma had kept her sewing machine (that worked by turning a handle) and her dressmaker's dummy, a slim lady with one leg and no head. She had gone to Gran's house, with Great Grandma. Dad had taken up the floorboards. He was going to put in water pipes and waste pipes, but he was also looking for woodworm.

'Tiny round holes,' he told Ken. 'That's what you want to look for.' Ken inspected every floorboard, and the joists that held them up, but he did not find a single hole.

'It's good wood,' Dad said. 'No rot, either. Lots of houses as old as this one were very badly built, but your great great grandad knew his business.'

'Great Grandma's father built this house?' Ken said. That was Pa, then, who had thrown away all the photographs of Kenny.

'Oh, yes,' said Dad. 'He helped to build all the houses in this street, and then he rented this one, and in the end, he bought it. When he died, he left it to his daughter. He was a builder too, a master carpenter. I expect he put down these floorboards himself. Now, can you fetch up that ratchet screwdriver I left in the hall?'

Ken went downstairs. The front door was always left open while they worked and the white cat from next door was asleep on the step. He was pleased to see it again, but it reminded him of how much

he missed being here with Great
Grandma, listening to the radio, looking
at the photographs and chatting about
school. These days, he had to be careful of
what he said.

On the last Friday of term they had the school sports and Ken won the obstacle race and the hundred metres, and came second in the hurdles. When he went round to Gran's that evening he told her about it, in a whisper, so that Great Grandma should not hear and start worrying about kings and queens again.

On Sunday he was back at Cedar Street with Dad, who was boasting about Ken to his friend John. Ken carried tools into the house and pretended not to hear.

John was an electrician. Dad planned to install a shower in the new bathroom, and John was putting in the wiring. Unfortunately, the bathroom was at the back of the house and the electricity meter at the front, so John took up some floorboards downstairs, and ran a cable through to the kitchen. Then he dug a groove in the plaster and sank the cable into the wall, up through the kitchen ceiling and into the bathroom. He did it very neatly, but when he left to go home he forgot to replace the floorboards over the hole underneath the electricity meter.

'I'll do it later,' Dad said. Ken knelt by the hole and peered in. His own house had concrete floors but there was a space

under Great Grandma's floor, about fifty centimetres deep and very dark, though he could just see little squares of light in the distance, which were the holes in the air bricks. He put his head right down into the hole. There was just room down there to crawl about, if he kept himself very flat, but he knew what Dad would have to say if he caught Ken fooling around, and it was not really worth the trouble. This wasn't the kind of house that had secret passages under it. Gran's house had a cellar, where Grandpa kept his home-made wine, but there was nothing very secret about it.

He was just coming out of the hole when something brushed his neck. He was so startled that he jumped and banged his head on the edge of a floorboard. Then he came out of the hole very fast. Could there be a ghost under the floor? Rats? Snakes? He looked round. Standing

beside him was the white cat from next
door. Its tail must have brushed his neck
as it walked round him.

'You frightened me,' Ken told it, but
the cat ignored him. It too was peering
into the hole, perhaps hoping for giant
mice.

He heard feet coming downstairs, hollowly, because the carpet had gone, and Dad looked in at the door.

'Just going back home to pick up some piping,' he said. 'Keep an eye on things. Won't be ten minutes,' and he hurried away round the corner to where the car was parked.

Ken noticed a scrabbling sound behind him and turned quickly in case something was climbing out of the hole. But that was not what was happening at all. The cat had vanished, and sticking out of the hole was a fat, furry white tail. As he watched, the tail disappeared, too.

Chapter 4

KEN PUT HIS head down the hole again and made the tweeting noises that cats seem to like. He didn't even know this cat's name. Great Grandma had called it Puss, or Kitty or Fluff, but the only word it seemed to know was milk.

There was no sound from the hole. Ken thought he could see something moving about in the darkness, but he could not be sure. Worse, he did not know how big that hole was. Did it end where the house ended, or did it go on and on, under all the houses, all the way down to Number 1, Cedar Street?

He called again, but nothing happened. Suppose the cat got lost, or stuck somewhere, trapped and starving. He couldn't just leave it.

Ken took another look down the hole. If he was very careful he could get himself down there; there was just about enough room. He started to lower his feet in, then realized that it would be easier if he went down head first. He lay flat on the floor, put his arms into the hole until his hands touched the ground, and then slowly

wriggled in after them.

It was very cramped there, under the floor, with no room even to move on

hands and knees. His fingers touched the
cable that John had laid, and he knew he
was lying on rubble, bits of brick and
cement and eighty-five years of dust, but
he could see nothing, so he lay there until
his eyes got used to the darkness.

It wasn't *quite* dark. There ahead of
him were the little squares of light from
the air bricks. He began to pull himself

towards them, coughing as the disturbed
dust swirled around his face and up his
nose, into his mouth. Suddenly the

nearer row of lights was blotted out. Something had moved in front of them. Something was with him down there in the darkness. For a moment he was ready to turn round and scramble out of the hole again, then he laughed. Of course: it was the cat.

As he pulled himself towards it he could see its eyes. Then he heard it purr. He came up alongside the airbricks and discovered that the cat had done what all

good cats do. It had curled up on a newspaper.

'Come on, you silly animal,' Ken said, tugging at the paper. The cat made an offended noise and walked off, stepping on his hand as it went and tickling his face with its fur. Ken turned his head to watch where it went and was in time to see it reach the patch of light behind him where the hole in the floor was. With one bound it leaped out and left him there.

Still clutching the newspaper, Ken turned very carefully so that the rubble should not make too many dents in him, and wriggled back to the hole. It was almost like being under the net in the obstacle race again, and getting out was harder than getting in. He had to turn on his back and slowly raise himself into a sitting position, using his arms as levers, until his head was out of the hole and he could rest his elbows on the floorboards either side. Then he heaved the rest of himself upright and stood in the hole. Last of all, he stepped out, next to the electricity meter. He laid the floorboards over the hole to keep the cat from getting in again and then saw Dad standing in the doorway.

'Can't leave you alone for five minutes, can I?' Dad complained. 'I'd have thought you'd have more sense. Suppose you'd hurt yourself down there? I wouldn't have known where you were, would I? I'd never have *guessed*.'

Ken explained about the cat.

'It would have come out by itself, anyway, I expect,' Dad said. 'Just think twice before you do anything like that again. Hey – what's that you've got there?'

Ken looked down at the floor. At his

feet lay the sheet of newspaper that the cat had been sitting on.

'Well, look at that,' Dad said, taking it from him. '20 November, 1907. It's the *Daily Mirror*. That's changed a bit, hasn't it?'

It wasn't a whole newspaper, just a double-page spread, with photographs.

'I didn't know they had newspaper photos in those days,' Ken said.

'You've got a museum piece there,'
Dad said. 'Just a minute, look at this.'

On the left hand side of the page was a
picture of a boy, in knickerbockers and a
peaked cap, standing beside a bicycle.
Underneath it said, *Kenneth Avery, aged*

*fourteen, of Tottenham, winner of the
Greenwich to Gravesend Road Race.*

'Well, that's one mystery solved,' Dad
said. 'That's Great Grandma's Kenny. He

won a cycling race.'

But Ken was looking at the photograph beside it, a picture of a lot of people, one row sitting, one row standing, wearing stiff clothes, long dresses, huge hats. And underneath that one it said:

Never before have so many kings, queens, princes and princesses been photographed at once as was the case on Sunday when twenty-four royalties were photographed by Mr William Downey at Windsor Castle.

'So that's it!' Ken cried. 'All the kings and queens of Europe.'

'Not *all*,' Dad said, 'but quite a lot. It tells you who they all are, look. Here's the King of England, and the Kaiser of Germany, behind him. Seven years later England and Germany were at war. And here's the Princess of Wales –'

'What, Princess Diana?' Ken said.

'In 1907? Come off it. No, this one became Queen Mary, our Queen's

58

Granny. Even *I* remember her,' Dad said. 'Just.'

'Fancy it being under the floor,' Ken said. 'And fancy us finding it, just when we needed it.'

'Not really so strange,' Dad said. 'When builders work on a house they often write their names and the date somewhere, or hide a newspaper – for other builders to find one day. I've done it myself.'

'Great Grandma said her dad had a special place for that picture,' Ken said. 'He must have forgotten about it when he got rid of the others.'

'I don't suppose he forgot,' Dad said. 'It's just that he didn't have to look at this one. I expect it was a secret comfort to him, knowing it was there. I'll tell you what, was there a photographer at your school sports?'

'Yes – from the *Courier*.'

'You're sure to be in the paper this time; properly, I mean, what with winning so much. When I put the floorboards back upstairs I'll hide a copy – for someone else to find in eighty-five years' time,' Dad said. 'Now, haven't you got somewhere to go with that picture?'

Ken dusted himself down and set out for Gran's house.

'Good heavens,' Gran said, when she saw him. 'What have you been up to?'

'Exploring,' Ken said. 'Where's Great Grandma? I've got something to show her.'

'In the garden,' Gran said. 'She may be dozing – don't make her jump.'

Great Grandma was not asleep. She was sitting in the sunshine with her stick beside her and she opened her eyes when Gran and Ken came down the garden.

'Hello, Kenny,' she said. 'I've been waiting for you.' Then she saw what he had in his hand. 'Is that the paper you've

got there?'

'Yes,' he said. 'Yes, Mary,' and he laid
it open on her lap. Great Grandma put on
her glasses and stared at the photographs
for a long, long while. At last she looked
up at Ken and Gran, and smiled.

'There you are,' she said, 'what did I tell
you? There's our Kenny, in the paper,
with all the kings and queens.'